About the Author

Faye Wolf is a young Dutch fashion designer born in London and raised in France. Her empire, Little Wolf, is a children's fashion brand based in LA/London for parents and kids based on the five vows that all the little wolves should follow.

She started writing stories from a very early age; she is very creative and full of imagination. Her clothing collections are just as unique as her stories and are available to purchase at the back of the book.

After growing up in different parts of the world, she has written many more stories to come. Inspired by beautiful events that have happened in her life. We welcome you to these magical stories and to be part of the little wolf pack and help us make this world a better place.

Love Faye Wolf

Dear Jere wade cook
i have heard that you are both 2
wonderful special amazing twins :)
I am very happy I can share with you
the stories of this magical jacket, there are
many more stories to come, and i hope you
enjoy them :) , this book is all about being
kind and making this world a better place.
which i am sure you both do :)

and when the summer comes i will send you
both a magical jacket

be good be safe be as great as you are
shine bright, and welcome to the little
wolf pack :)

Little Wolf
The Story of Little J

Faye Wolf
Illustrations by Veronika Caskova

Little Wolf
The Story of Little J

Nightingale Books

NIGHTINGALE PAPERBACK

© Copyright 2022
Faye Wolf
Illustrations by Veronika Caskova

A CIP catalogue record for this title is
available from the British Library.
ISBN 9781838750428

Nightingale Books is an imprint of
Pegasus Elliot MacKenzie Publishers Ltd.
www.pegasuspublishers.com

First Published in 2022

Nightingale Books
Sheraton House Castle Park
Cambridge England

Printed & Bound in Great Britain

Each jacket is magically made and you will be able to purchase a magical jacket and become part of the little wolf pack on our website at the following: Littlewolfkids.com and please follow us on Instagram @littlewolfkids @iamfayewolf

One day there was a little boy called Little J
who had a best friend called Vivi.

They lived in a big city full of lights and Little
J's main wish was to help others.

So every day he would do a good deed.

After getting dressed and walking to school he would always make someone smile.

But one day something changed.

While he was walking home after school with Vivi
they both saw bright lights in the bushes.

So they ran to them...

And discover it was a magical jacket lost in the leaves with a little wolf on the back glowing bright.

"Wow!!!" said Vivi out loud. "I think this jacket is magical. What do we do?"

Little Wolf
VOWS

1. Love and accept myself.

2. Treat others the way I wish to be treated.

3. Be kind to animals and help others.

4. Follow my dreams.

5. Make a difference in the world.

As they picked it up, they saw that inside the jacket there were five vows.

They gazed in amazement.

"Oh my gosh," said Vivi. "What is this? Read it, Little J!"

So Little J read them out.

"Five vows
1. Love and accept myself.
2. Treat others the way
I want to be treated.
3. Be kind to animals.
4. Follow my dreams.
5. Make a difference
in the world."

And that's when Little J knew this jacket was magical and they both must help the world with these five vows.

In excitement they both ran home.

Once home they both went upstairs and decided to hide it so his parents wouldn't see it, and named it little wolf.

Later that night while Little J was hiding under the covers, he couldn't stop staring at his closet watching the glowing lights from underneath.

Slowly he fell asleep.

The next morning Little J woke up really excited and happy and couldn't wait to wear his magical jacket.

He rushed out of the house to pick up his best friend and went to school.

During the day he saw a bird that had fallen
out of a tree and broken her wing.

And as we must be kind to animals, he helped the little bird and gently touched her wing and magically it was better.

The little birdie said,
"Thank you," and flew away.

As days went by everything became better.

Everything he touched became better. The bullying at school had also stopped and everyone was kind to each other.

Little J turned round and said, "Yes, I know it is the jacket, it really is magical."

He gazed in amazement watching everyone he had healed and helped.

Magical things happened every day and when he helped his friends and the animals his magical powers got stronger.

So every night he hid the jacket in his closet.

Until one night he was fast asleep and his mother saw the glowing light from under the door and walked in while he was sleeping and found the little wolf jacket.

In the early morning Little J woke up in a panic
and worry after seeing it wasn't there.

He ran downstairs yelling, "Mummy, Mummy my jacket is gone."

His mummy looked at him and said, "Don't worry my darling, I have it, but what is so special about this jacket?"

"Mummy, I will show you," he said.

He then ran outside with the jacket on and yelled, "Mummy, look."

As she looked he went to one of her flowers in the garden only to see them bloom and become bigger and brighter.

His mummy stood in shock watching as his jacket was glowing. She said, "I have never seen a magical jacket like this."

Little J gushed and said, "I know, Mummy. It helps people and makes them happy, it has stopped the bullying at school, helped animals and everyone is to now kind to each other."

So every night Little J put his jacket back in the closet while he sleeps, ready to wake up, save lives and make this world a better place with his magical jacket.

But he was still questioning whether this was
the only little wolf jacket out there?

To be continued...

LiTTLE WoLF

I _____, confirm that I am now a member of the " The Little wolf pack" and I agree to obey all the Little wolf rules.

I pledge to follow and support the Little wolf movement to help make this world a better place.

My family and I are happy to belong to the "Little wolf pack", and be a part of this beautiful adventure.

Date: _____   Signature:_____